D1465478

C016328899

This book belongs to:

. . . .

. . . .

Quarto is the authority on a wide range of topics.

Quarto educates, entertains and enriches the lives of
our readers—enthusiasts and lovers of hands-on living.

www.quartoknows.com

Designer: Chris Fraser
Series Designer: Victoria Kimonidou

Copyright © QED Publishing 2017
First published in the UK in 2017
by QED Publishing
Part of The Quarto Group
The Old Brewery
6 Blundell Street
London, N7 9BH

A catalogue record for this book is available from the British Library.

ISBN 978 1 78493 727 0

Printed in China

The Girl Who Cried Wolf!

Written by Steve Smallman
Illustrated by Neil Price

"**T**HIS IS SO BORING!" screeched Princess Arabella, throwing her knitting on the floor.

"What is?" asked her maid.
"Everything! Being a princess is boring!" she replied.

Princess Arabella stomped over to the window and looked outside.

A shepherd boy was sitting in the sunshine watching his sheep and looking ridiculously happy.

The princess suddenly had an idea...

Tom the shepherd boy was shocked when he saw the princess and her soldiers marching up the hill towards him.

Trembling, Tom knelt down in the mud.

"We are swapping jobs!" announced Princess Arabella. "From now on I will be the shepherd and you... will be the prince!"

"The prince?" cried Tom. "But I don't know how to be a prince!"

"Oh it's not hard," chuckled Arabella. "Tell me, what does a shepherd do?"

"Well, you look after the sheep. And if a wolf comes along, shout "WOLF, WOLF!" as loud as you can and the townsfolk will come to help you." replied Tom.

"Ooh, how exciting!" cried Arabella.

So 'Prince' Tom was dragged off to the castle. Meanwhile Arabella the shepherd sat down on a log to watch the sheep.

She watched them and watched them. But the sheep didn't do anything except eat and poop, and there was no sign of a wolf.

Soon Arabella was bored, so she decided
to play a trick on the townsfolk.

"WOLF, WOLF!"
she screamed at the
top of her voice.

In minutes, all the townsfolk came rushing up the hill,
waving forks and flaming torches to scare away the wolf.

"Princess, are you
alright?" cried one
of the men.

"I'm not a princess, you silly man, I'm a shepherd!"
Arabella snapped. "If you want to speak to royalty, talk to
the new prince. He'll be having a bubble bath about now."

"Oh, sorry, your high... I mean shepherd... ness,"
stuttered the man. "But where's the wolf?"

"Oh, it seems to have gone now,"
Arabella said sweetly. "Off you pop!
Thanks for coming!"

"She's telling lies!"
Tom shouted angrily.
"There wasn't a wolf!"

"I stink of roses! Can I go back to being a shepherd now?" Tom asked the maid.

"Oh no, sir," said the maid. "It's time to ride your new pony!"

"But I hate ponies," cried Tom.
"I only like sheep!"

Arabella, still chuckling to herself, went back to watching the sheep. But it wasn't long before she was bored again...

"BEAR, BEAR!" she cried as loudly as she could.

In a few minutes, all the people from the town came rushing up the hill, red-faced and out of breath.

"Where's the bear?"
gasped the townsfolk.

"Oh, you were too slow,"
giggled Arabella.

The townsfolk didn't
believe her and wandered
back, muttering crossly.

"She's lying again!" cried
Prince Tom who was being
forced to eat fancy food.

"I really wish I could
go back to my old job,"
he sighed.

Arabella soon got bored again and this time she shouted, "TROLL, TROLL!" at the top of her voice.

The townsfolk came puffing back up the hill, looking hot and puzzled.

"Where's the troll?" they asked.

"Oh, I scared it away," cackled Arabella. "I poked it with a long stick."

"So where is it now?" they asked.

"Oh, it'll be over that hill by now. It was a very fast troll, with... er... running shoes on," Arabella replied.

The townsfolk didn't believe her at all and angrily stomped back down the hill.

Back at the castle,
Prince Tom had
a visit from the
townsfolk.
They'd had
enough of
Arabella's lies.

"But what can I do?" cried Tom.
"I can't make her tell the truth!"

"No, but as a prince you
can decide whether we
should run to help every
time she shouts 'wolf' or
'bear' or whatever it is
next,"said the townsfolk.

"Well," smiled Prince Tom,
"I think you should ignore
the new shepherd next time.
She's told too many lies."

"Yes, Your Highness!"
the townsfolk replied, bowing low.

Sure enough, a few minutes later there
came another shout from the hill...

"DRAGON, DRAGON!"

"Whatever will she think of next?" sighed the townsfolk.
They all ignored her and carried on with what they were doing.

But Tom had seen the dragon from the castle window and was already running as fast as he could up the hill.

He grabbed a bucket full of water and threw it right in the face of the huge dragon.

The dragon flew away coughing and sneezing.

"That was AMAZING!" said Arabella.
"You fought off a dragon all by yourself!
Where are all the townsfolk?"

"You told so many
lies that when you
finally told the truth
nobody believed
you," said Tom.

"I'm really sorry Tom. Thank you
for saving me," replied Arabella. "Do you
think we should swap jobs again?"

"YES!" said Tom.
"You're a useless shepherd!"

"I know," laughed Arabella. "I much
prefer being a princess."

And from that day on, whenever Arabella
was tempted to tell a lie, she thought of the
terrifying dragon... and instead told the truth.

Next Steps

Show the children the cover again. When they first saw it, did they think that they already knew the story? How is this story different from the traditional story? Which parts are the same?

Why did Princess Arabella want to be a shepherd? Did Tom want to be a prince?

When Arabella cried "WOLF, WOLF!" was she telling the truth? Ask the children why they think Arabella lied.

All the townsfolk came rushing to help Arabella to scare off the wolf. How do you think the townsfolk felt when they realised there wasn't a wolf? Ask the children to imagine how they would feel if somebody told them a lie like that.

Ask the children if they can remember what else Arabella shouted. Did the townsfolk believe her? Discuss whether it is ever alright to tell a lie.

When Arabella shouted "DRAGON, DRAGON!" why didn't the townsfolk run to help her?

Tom was very brave when he faced the dragon all on his own. What would have happened to the sheep if he hadn't been there? What could have happened to Arabella?

Ask the children to draw a wolf, bear, troll or a big, scary, fire-breathing dragon!